WAG-BY-WALL

BY
BEATRIX POTTER ™

Illustrated by
PAULINE BAYNES

FREDERICK WARNE

FREDERICK WARNE

Penguin Books Ltd, Harmondsworth, Middlesex, England
Viking Penguin Inc., 40 West 23rd Street, New York, New York 10010, U.S.A.
Penguin Books Australia Ltd, Ringwood, Victoria, Australia
Penguin Books Canada Limited, 2801 John Street, Markham, Ontario, Canada L3R 1B4
Penguin Books (N.Z.) Ltd, 182–190 Wairau Road, Auckland 10, New Zealand

First published in the U.S.A. by The Horn Book, Inc., 1944
First published in Great Britain by Frederick Warne & Co., 1944
This edition first published 1987
Copyright © Frederick Warne & Co., 1944, 1971, 1987

ISBN 0 7232 3448 5

Typeset by CCC, printed and bound in Great Britain by
William Clowes Limited, Beccles and London

WAG-BY-WALL

INTRODUCTION

THE story of *Wag-by-Wall* dates back to November 1909, and at that time it was called *The Little Black Kettle*. The middle part of this story is unfinished, and the songs sung by the little black kettle and others are only roughly sketched in, but at least they show Beatrix Potter's method of planning her verses. "I remember", said Beatrix Potter many years later, "Sally's story stuck because the kettle was obstinately dumb."

The old woman was Sally Scales who lived at Stott Farm in the woods, about a mile from Graythwaite, from where many of the Hill Top pigs were bought. She was very knowledgeable about cows and pigs.

This unfinished story of 1909 was then put on one side and it was not touched again until 1929, when it was rewritten as a part of *The Fairy Caravan*—but it was eventually taken out of *The Fairy Caravan* manuscript and never published in that form.

Another ten or more years passed, and then towards the end of 1940 Bertha Miller asked if she might print the story in *The Horn Book Magazine*, suggesting that it could be made into a Christmas story with its setting on Christmas Eve. In response to her request Beatrix Potter again rewrote it, this time leaving out all references to her Fairy Caravan characters.

In November 1941 in a letter to Mrs. Miller, she referred to the story saying: "I cannot judge my own work. Is not *Wag-by-the-Wa*' rather a pretty story if divested of the 'Jenny Ferret' rubbish? I thought of it years ago as a pendant to *The Tailor of Gloucester*—the lonely old man and the lonely old woman; but I never could finish it all."

Mrs. Miller decided that she would like to hold back the story for the twentieth anniversary number of *The Horn Book Magazine*, and on November 5th 1943, Beatrix Potter wrote again saying, "I cordially agree with the delay until May for printing the story in the Horn Book. It

5

leaves time to see proofs, and I would like to make it as nearly word-perfect as I know how, for the credit of your 20th anniversary. The winter's snow will be over by then. Would you desire to drop 'Christmas Eve?' I am inclined to leave it *in*, with perhaps an added sentiment about the return of spring—(How the sad world longs for it!) I liked your suggestion of Christmas Eve because I like to think some of your story tellers may read the story, turn about with the old *Tailor of Gloucester* at Christmas gatherings in the children's libraries." Beatrix Potter never saw the final proofs, however, for seven weeks later she died.

(From *A History of the Writings of
Beatrix Potter*, by Leslie Linder)

ONCE upon a time there was an old woman called Sally Benson who lived alone in a little thatched cottage. She had a garden and two fields, and there was grazing for a cow on the bog in summer, while the fields were shut off to grow hay-grass.

When her husband was alive, and able to work, they had lived comfortably. He worked for a farmer, while Sally milked the cow and fed their pig at home. After Sally became a widow she had a hard struggle. Tom Benson's long illness had left debts.

The cottage had belonged to Sally's mother, and to her grandparents before her. Her grandfather had been a cattle dealer. He bought and sold cattle at fairs, and made a bit of money. Nobody knew what he had done with it. He did not seem to spend much; and he never gave away one farthing.

The old furniture was poor and plain; the only handsome piece that had belonged to the old man was "Wag-by-Wall", the clock.

"Tic : toc : gold : toes : tic : toc : gold : toes :" it repeated over and over, till anybody might have felt provoked to throw a shoe at it. "Tic : toc : gold : toes :"

Sally took no notice. The clock had been saying those words ever since she was born. Nobody knew what it meant. Sally thought the world of the clock; and she loved her old singing kettle. She boiled water to make balm tea. She made it in a jug, and she grew the lemon-scented balm in her own garden.

The kettle had been cracked and mended more than once. The last time Sally took it to the smithy, Isaac Blacksmith looked at it over his spectacles and said, "More patch than bottom. It will cost you more than a new kettle."

"Nay, Nay! thou mun patch it, Isaac Blacksmith! I tell thee, thou mun patch it; and thou mun patch it again!" Sally stood on tiptoes to whisper, "I tell thee, it can sing."

"Aye, aye? like a toom barrel?" said Isaac Blacksmith, blowing the bellows.

SO Sally went on using her old kettle, and it sang to her. The kettle sang on the hearth; and the bees sang in the garden, where she grew old-fashioned flowers as well as potatoes and cabbages. There were wallflowers and pansies and roses in their seasons; balm for her own herb tea; and thyme, hyssop, and borage that the honeybees love.

When Sally sat knitting by the cottage door, she listened to the bees. "Arise, work : pray : Night follows day. Sweet summer's day." The bees hummed drowsily amongst the flowers. "To bed with sun. Day's work well done." The bees went home into their hives at dusk.

Presently indoors the kettle began to sing. At first it sang gently and slowly, then faster and faster and louder and louder, as it came to boiling and bubbling over. It sang words something like this— to the tune of Ash Grove—

With pomp, power, and glory the world beckons vainly,
  In chase of such vanities why should I roam?
While peace and content bless my little thatched cottage
  And warm my own hearth with the treasures of Home.

Sally Benson sitting by her fire on a winter's evening listened to the kettle's song, and she was contented. The cottage was warm and dry; it was whitewashed without and within, and spotlessly clean. There was no upstairs; only the kitchen, with cupboards and a box bed in the wall; and behind the kitchen was another tiny room and a pantry. Sally thought the cottage was a palace. She had no wish to live in a big house.

Above the kitchen hearth, at the south end of the cottage, there was a tall stone chimney stack standing up above the roof. Dry thatch is dangerous for catching fire from sparks ; but there was plenty of green moss and houseleeks growing beside Sally Benson's chimney. Under the same long low roof, at the north end, was a woodshed.

A PAIR of white owls lived in the shed. Every summer, year after year, they nested there—though it could scarcely be called a "nest"! The hen owl just laid four white eggs on a bare board under the rafters. The little owlets were like balls of fluff, with big dark eyes. The youngest owlet, that hatched out of the last-laid egg, was always smaller than the others. Sally called him "Benjamin".

When the owlets were old enough, they came out onto the thatch; they climbed up and sat in a row on the ridge of the roof. They hissed, and craned their necks and twisted their heads to watch their parents mousing over the bog. The old owls flitted noiselessly over the long coarse grass and rushes; they looked like great white moths in the twilight.

As the young owlets grew older they grew more and more hungry ; the mother owl used to come out hunting food by day-light in the afternoons. The peewits over the bog swooped down at her, crying and wailing, although she was only searching for mice.

Little breezes stirred the cotton grass and wildflowers; and Nancy Cow, knee-deep in sedge and meadowsweet, blew warm breath lazily. Her big feet squelched amongst moss and eyebright and sundew; she turned back to firm turf and lay down to wait until Sally's voice called her home for milking.

When the old owls brought mice, they fed each wide gaping mouth in turn. Amongst the jostling and hissing and snatching, Benjamin was often knocked over. Sometimes he rolled down the thatch and fell off the roof. Sally picked him up and lifted him back again. If the night had been wet, she dried him by the fire.

One morning she found all four baby owlets huddled on the doorstep hissing at the cat.

Sally was very fond of the owls. Indeed she was fond of all things; a smiling, friendly old woman with cheeks like withered apples.

But "good times and hard times—all times go over". While the hard times lasted they hit poor Sally very hard. There came a year of famine. Rain spoilt the hay and harvest; blight ruined the potato crop. Sally's pig died, and she was forced to sell her cow to pay the debts. There seemed to be nothing left but to sell the cottage also, and end her days in the poorhouse. She had nobody that she could turn to; no one to ask for help.

She and Tom had lost their only child, a daughter. Such a dear pretty girl she had been, with yellow curls, rosy cheeks, and blue eyes always laughing, until she ran away to marry a wastrel. Sally had sent money when a baby girl was born ; another little "Goldie-locks". Time and again they wrote for money. When Sally had no more to send they faded out of sight.

ON Christmas Eve, Sally Benson sat by the fire reading a letter which the postman had brought her. It was a sad letter, written by a stranger. It said that her daughter and her son-in-law were dead, and that a neighbour—the writer of the letter—had taken their child into her home out of pity.

"A bonny child she is; a right little 'Goldie-locks'; eight years old, and tidy and helpful. She will be a comfort to her Grannie. Please send money for her journey and I will set her on her way. I cannot keep her long; I have five mouths to feed. Please send the money soon, Mrs. Benson."

Poor Sally! with no money, and no prospect but the poorhouse. That Christmas Eve in the moonlight, a white owl sat on the chimney stack. When a cloud came over the moon, the owl dozed. Perhaps a wisp of blue smoke floating upwards made him sleepy. He swayed forward and fell into the chimney.

Down below Sally Benson sat by the hearth, watching the dying fire. One hand crumpled the letter in the pocket of her old black skirt; the other thin trembling hand was twisted in her apron. Tears ran down her poor old nose; she mopped them with her apron. She was not crying for her daughter whose troubles were over. She was crying for little Goldie-locks.

She sat on and on into the night. At length there was a noise high up inside the chimney. There came a rush of soot and stones; small stones and bits of mortar came first. Several large heavy stones tumbled after; and the white owl followed on top of them.

"Save us! what a dirty mess!" said Sally, scrambling to her feet and forgetting her troubles.

She picked up the owl gently, and blew the soot off him. The soft feather tip of one wing was scorched; otherwise he was unhurt. But soot had got into his eyes and gullet; he blinked and gasped and choked. Sally fetched milk and fed him with a spoon.

Then she turned to sweep up the mess on the hearth. There was a smell of charred wood and burning wool. Amongst the stones was a black thing that smoked. It was an old stocking tied round the ankle with a bit of string. The foot was full of something heavy. Gold pieces shone through a hole in the toes.

"Tic : toc : gold : toes!" said Wag-by-Wall, the clock. Something seemed to have happened to Wag-by-Wall; it went whirr whirra whrrr! trying to strike. When it struck at last, it struck fourteen instead of twelve, and changed its tick. Instead of saying "tic : toc : gold : toes :" it said, "Tick er tocks : Goldie-locks" and those were its words ever after.

☆

Sally Benson fetched her little grand-daughter to live with her. She bought another cow, and a pig; and she grew potatoes and balm and sweet flowers in her garden for the bees. And every summer white owls nested in the woodshed.

Sally enjoyed a cheerful contented old age, and little Goldie-locks grew up and married a young farmer. They lived happily ever after, and they always kept the singing kettle and Wag-by-Wall, the clock.